The Adventures of
BERT

ALLAN AHLBERG & RAYMOND BRIGGS

VIKING

VIKING

Published by the Penguin Group
Penguin Books Ltd, 27 Wrights Lane, London W8 5TZ, England
Penguin Putnam Inc., 375 Hudson Street, New York, New York 10014, USA
Penguin Books Australia Ltd, Ringwood, Victoria, Australia
Penguin Books Canada Ltd, 10 Alcorn Avenue, Toronto, Ontario, Canada M4V 3B2
Penguin Books India (P) Ltd, 11 Community Centre, Panchsheel Park, New Delhi – 110 017, India
Penguin Books (NZ) Ltd, Cnr Rosedale and Airborne Roads, Albany, Auckland, New Zealand
Penguin Books (South Africa) (Pty) Ltd, 5 Watkins Street, Denver Ext 4, Johannesburg 2094, South Africa

On the World Wide Web at: www.penguin.com

Penguin Books Ltd, Registered Offices: Harmondsworth, Middlesex, England

First published 2001
3 5 7 9 10 8 6 4 2

Text copyright © Allan Ahlberg, 2001
Illustrations copyright © Raymond Briggs, 2001

The moral right of the author and illustrator has been asserted

Set in Bembo

Printed in Italy by L.E.G.O.

British Library Cataloguing in Publication Data
A CIP catalogue record for this book is available from the British Library

ISBN 0–670–89329–3

CHAPTER ONE

Bert

Meet Bert.
This is him.
Say hallo to Bert.

Meet Mrs Bert.
This is her.
Say hallo to her
as well.

Hallo!

Meet Baby Bert.
Don't say hallo to him.
He is fast asleep.

Shh!
Turn the page ... quietly.

Oh no!
Now look what you've done.

CHAPTER TWO

Bert and the Shirt

One day Bert has
an adventure with a shirt.

Here is the shirt.
Do you like it?

Bert puts
the shirt on.
It gets stuck
over his head.

He falls downstairs.

He rolls into the street.

He rolls into a lorry.

He ends up in Scotland.

Poor Bert!

BAAA!

CHAPTER THREE

Bert and the Sausage

The next day Bert has
an adventure with a sausage.

Bert is out shopping.
He sees a sausage in the street.

Bert runs off.

The sausage chases him.

Bert falls over.

Bert bangs his nose.

But it is only a man in a sausage suit,
selling sausages.
The sausage man helps Bert to his feet.
He gives him his hat back
... and a free sausage.

Lucky Bert!

CHAPTER FOUR

Bert and the Cardboard Box

The *next* day Bert has
an adventure with a cardboard box.

Bert is walking by the river.
He sees a cardboard box go floating by.
There it is – look!

The box is big and brown
... and *barking*.

WOOF! WOOF! WOOF!

Bert dives in
to rescue the box.

Then he remembers –
he can't swim.

Bert splashes!

Bert shouts!

Bert sinks!

Bert ... stands up.

The water is not as deep as he thought.

Bert lies on the bank.

A *puppy* creeps out of the box.

He licks Bert's face.

Bert is his hero.

Brave Bert!

CHAPTER
FIVE

Goodnight, Bert!

It is bedtime now.
Bert is in his pyjamas.
Say goodnight to Bert.

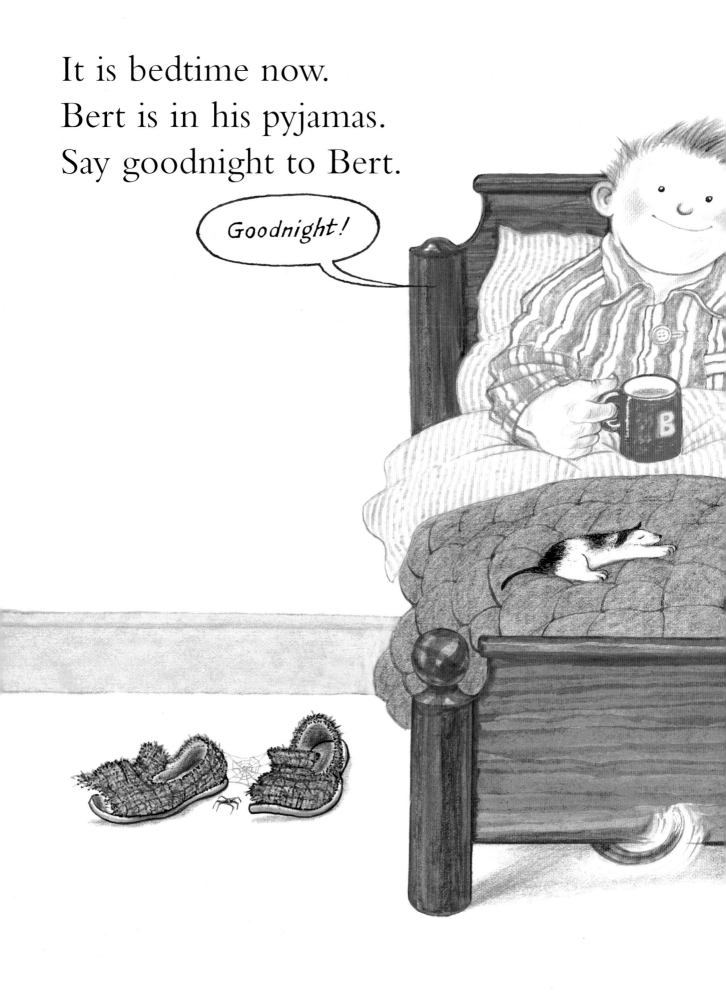

Goodnight!

Mrs Bert is in her pyjamas.
Say goodnight to her as well.

Goodnight !

Baby Bert
is in his cot.
Don't say goodnight
to him.
Don't make a sound.

Shh!
Turn the page
very, very ... quietly.

Oh no!
You've done it again!

The End